STUCK

OLIVER JEFFERS

PHILOMEL BOOKS
An Imprint of Penguin Group (USA) Inc.

To those who were there - Papa, Rosebud, Davebud, the Brother, the Other Brother, Arn, Chester and San.

PHILOMEL BOOKS

A division of Penguin Young Readers Group.
Published by The Penguin Group.
Penguin Group (USA) Inc., 375 Hudson Street, New York, NY 10014, U.S.A.
Penguin Group (Canada), 90 Eglinton Avenue East, Suite 700, Toronto, Ontario M4P 2Y3, Canada
(a division of Pearson Penguin Canada Inc.).
Penguin Books Ltd, 80 Strand, London WC2R 0RL, England.
Penguin Ireland, 25 St. Stephen's Green, Dublin 2, Ireland (a division of Penguin Books Ltd).
Penguin Group (Australia), 250 Camberwell Road, Camberwell, Victoria 3124, Australia
(a division of Pearson Australia Group Pty Ltd).
Penguin Books India Pvt Ltd, 11 Community Centre, Panchsheel Park, New Delhi - 110 017, India.
Penguin Group (NZ), 67 Apollo Drive, Rosedale, Auckland 0632, New Zealand (a division of Pearson New Zealand Ltd).
Penguin Books (South Africa) (Pty) Ltd, 24 Sturdee Avenue, Rosebank, Johannesburg 2196, South Africa.
Penguin Books Ltd, Registered Offices: 80 Strand, London WC2R 0RL, England.

Manufactured in China. The art for *Stuck* was created by compositing various scribbles and blotches of paint, made on small pieces of paper, all together inside my computer. This is because I needed to move studios in the middle of making the art, and using this approach seemed like a good idea.
Library of Congress Cataloging-in-Publication Data
Jeffers, Oliver. Stuck / Oliver Jeffers. p. cm.
Summary: When Floyd's kite gets stuck in a tree, he tries to knock it down with increasingly larger and more outrageous things.
[1. Humorous stories.] I. Title. PZ7.J3643St 2011 [E]—dc23 2011016349
ISBN 978-0-399-25737-7
9 10

IT ALL BEGAN

When Floyd's kite became stuck in A TREE.
He tried pulling and swinging, but it
WOULDN'T COME UNSTUCK.

The trouble **REALLY** began

when he threw his **FAVORITE SHOE**
to knock the kite loose...

...and THAT got stuck too!

So he threw up his other shoe
to knock down his FAVORITE one ...
and, UNBELievably,
that got STUCK as well.

In order to knock down
his other shoe,

Floyd fetched Mitch.

CATS get STUCK in trees
all the time, but this
WAS GETTING RIDICULOUS.

Floyd fetched
a ladder.

He was going to sort this out
once and FOR ALL...

...and up he threw it.

I'm sure you can
guess what happened.

The ladder was borrowed
from a neighbor and
would DEFINITELY
need to be put back before
anyone noticed...

and in order to do so.
Floyd FLUNG a BUCKET of
PAINT at it.

And wouldn't you know it....
the Bucket of paint got STUCK.

Then Floyd tried....

a duck to
knock down the
bucket of paint...

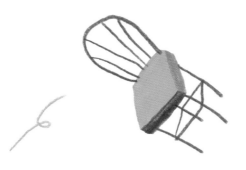

a chair
to knock down
the duck...

his friend's bicycle
to knock down
the chair...

The kitchen sink to knock down his friend's bicycle...

Floyd's front door to knock down the kitchen sink.

the FAMILY car
to knock down
their front door...

the
MILKMAN
to knock down
the Family car...

an orangutan to KNOCK DOWN
the milkman, who surely had
somewhere else to be...

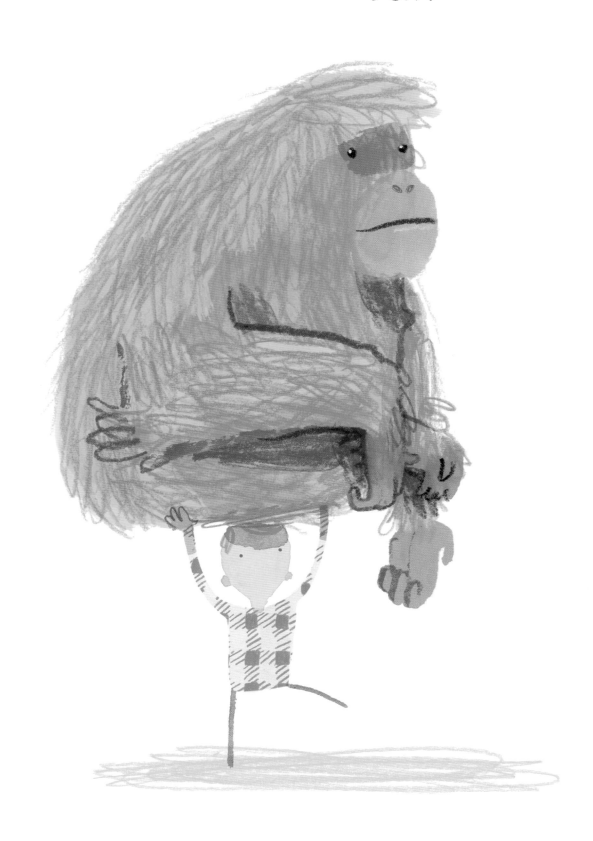

a small boat
to knock down
the orangutan...

a BIG
BOAT
to knock
down the
small
boat...

A ~~big~~ RHINOCEROS
to knock down
the BIG boat...

a long-distance TRUCK
to knock down the
rhinoceros...

the HOUSE across
the street
to knock down the
long-distance TRUCK...

FLOYD?

A LIGHThouse to KNOCK DOWN the house no longer across the street...

a curious whale, in THE
WRONG PLACE at THE WRONG TIME,
to knock down the lighthouse...

and they
ALL
GOT
STUCK.

A Fire Engine was passing
and heard all the COMMOTION.
The Firemen stopped to see
if they could help at all.

And up they went...
first the engine,

followed by the firemen, one by one.

And there they stayed,
stuck between the orangutan
and one of the BOATS.

Firemen would DEFINITELY
be noticed missing, and
Floyd KNEW he'd be in
BIG TROUBLE!

Then he had
an idea,

and went to
find a SAW.

He lined it
up as best he could...

...and HURLED IT UP THE TREE.

And that was it!
There was no more
room left in the
tree and the kite
came **unstuck.**

Floyd was delighted. He had
forgotten all about his kite
and put it to use immediately,
enjoying the rest of his DAY
very much.

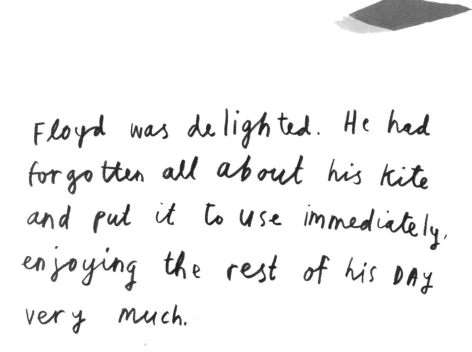

That night, Floyd fell asleep exhausted.
Though before he did, he could have sworn
there was something he was forgetting.